מוסיקה

ArtScroll® Uncle Moishy Series

Rabbi Nosson Scherman / Rabbi Gedaliah Zlotowitz
General Editors

Rabbi Meir Zlotowitz ז"ל, *Founder*

UNGLE MOISHY

The Very Best Pesach Surprise

Created by **Libby Lazewnik**
Written by **Perry Binet**

Published by
ARTSCROLL
Mesorah Publications, ltd

UNCLE MOISHY

THANK YOU

Rivky Robi Photography

The Wiederman Family

The Kohn Family

The Uncle Moishy World Team

Eli Kroen

Chaya Felsinger

Malky Schick

Doni Gross

RTSCROLL® UNCLE MOISHY SERIES

UNCLE MOISHY – THE VERY BEST PESACH SURPRISE

© *Copyright 2022 by* Mesorah Publications, Ltd.

First impression: March 2022

Published by **MESORAH PUBLICATIONS, LTD.**

313 Regina Avenue / Rahway, N.J. 07065 / (718) 921-9000 / Fax: (718) 680-1875 / www.artscroll.com

Photography by **Rivky Robi Photography**

Layout and design by **Eli Kroen and Aviva Kohn**

Distributed in Israel by **SIFRIATI / A. GITLER**
POB 2351 / Bnei Brak 51122 / Israel

Distributed in Europe by **LEHMANNS**
Unit E, Viking Business Park, Rolling Mill Road / Jarrow, Tyne and Wear / England NE32 3DP

Distributed in Australia and New Zealand by **GOLDS WORLD OF JUDAICA**
3-13 William Street / Balaclava, Melbourne 3183, Victoria, Australia

Distributed in South Africa by **KOLLEL BOOKSHOP**
Northfield Centre / 17 Northfield Avenue / Glenhazel 2192 / Johannesburg, South Africa

Printed in United States of America

ISBN-10: 1-4226-3092-7 / ISBN-13: 978-1-4226-3092-1

UNCLE MOISHY

Hi, boys and girls....

Hello, again. It's me, your favorite uncle...Uncle Moishy!

I'm so excited to be back again with a brand-new book and a new story that I'm sure you'll love!

In this story, we get to meet Meir and Malka, whose mother had twin babies! Wow! Mazel tov!

But Pesach was coming...and there was so, so much to be done! Who would do it all while Mommy took care of the babies?

Come along with me as I join Meir and Malka in preparing for Pesach. We had tons of fun, while learning many important lessons about the Yom Tov of Pesach.

From working together, to being mevater, to zrizus, to the mitzvah of hashavas aveidah, to responsibility, Meir and Malka learned many things...while making a huge surprise for Mommy!

Hashem is so proud of us when we work together, doing what we should, and helping out whenever we can. Always be sure to ask your parents how you can help before Yom Tov. You'll be doing a great mitzvah!

So enjoy...and have a happy Pesach!

Until next time,

Uncle Moishy

Unclemoishyworld.com • 844.4.UNCLEMOISHY
info@unclemoishyworld.com

Mazel Tov! Excitement filled the air,
Balloons and gifts were everywhere!
How special! Meir and Malka's mother
Came home, with two babies, a sister and brother.
But Pesach is coming tomorrow at night,
So much to be done. Can we get it all right?

Mommy and Abba worked for weeks before,
Shopping and cooking and so much more.
They bought us shoes and clothing all new,
Exciting fun toys, for Pesach, too!
Now, Mommy needs rest. The twins need their care,
Who will finish up? Who will prepare?

Malka whispered into Meir's ear,
"We need a plan to help Mommy so dear,
We'll finish it up. We'll do what we can.
Abba, please come. Let's make a plan!
We'll all work together. We'll all do our part,
We'll get this done quickly. Who's ready to start?"

"Let's go," said Abba, as he picked up a broom.
He began to hum, while he swept the room.
Malka and Meir scrubbed like never before,
When suddenly they heard a knock at the door.

They opened the door and who would have thought,
Uncle Moishy was there! And look what he brought!
"Mazel tov! I heard the great news,
Here's Pesach food, I'm sure you can use!
I'm here to help. Let's start right away!"
"Wow!" said Meir, "You just saved the day!"

"Let's turn on the music, get the playroom clean,
Let's vacuum the crumbs so they're not seen.
With Pesach coming in just one day,
We'll get rid of the chametz right away!"

The children began to clean and sing.
Uncle Moishy's songs had that special ring!

So many toys to make all neat,
How will this ever be complete?

Uncle Moishy smiled, "I'll teach you a trick:
To get the work done quicker than quick...
Whenever we start, we do things one by one,
And before you know it, the work is all done!"

Then Meir checked his school bag. His Haggadah was not there!
"Where can it be? How come it's not here?"
"Don't worry," Uncle Moishy said with great care,
"As we continue we'll find it somewhere."

"There's silver to be polished, let's make it shine.
We have so many nice cups, for grape juice and wine.
We want the Seder table to be as pretty as can be
As we celebrate the day that we were set free."

As they polished, Uncle Moishy said, "You're both smart,
Tell me something about Pesach — who's ready to start?"

"Me, first!" Malka cried. "Please listen to me!"
"No, me!" Meir shouted, as loud as could be.

"You both want to be heard with such great things to say.
But both going first is not the right way.
Here's a chance to be mevater and step aside,
When we let others go first, Hashem's filled with pride!"
"Okay," Meir said, "Malka, you go ahead."
"No," said Malka, "You go instead."

18

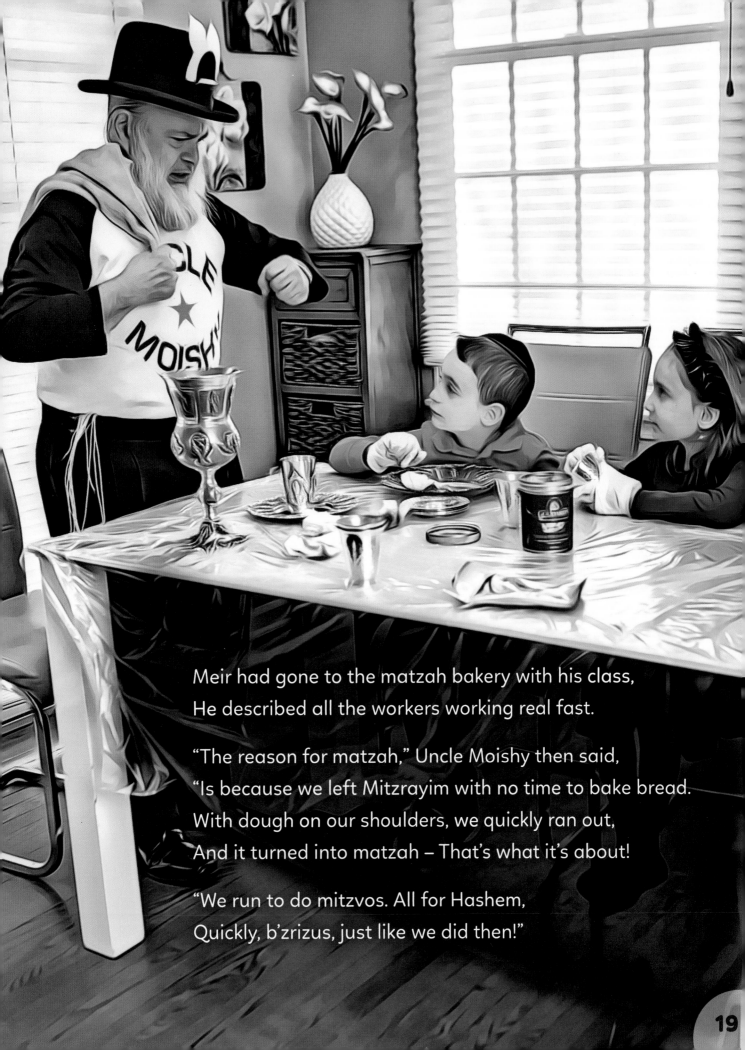

Meir had gone to the matzah bakery with his class,
He described all the workers working real fast.

"The reason for matzah," Uncle Moishy then said,
"Is because we left Mitzrayim with no time to bake bread.
With dough on our shoulders, we quickly ran out,
And it turned into matzah – That's what it's about!

"We run to do mitzvos. All for Hashem,
Quickly, b'zrizus, just like we did then!"

In the land of Mitzrayim, many years ago,
Lived a wicked king, Pharaoh, who was so mean — oh no!
"In my land called Mitzrayim, every Jew's now a slave!
It will be forever! Not one will be saved!"

"The work is too hard," the people all moaned.
They cried out to Hashem. The Jews all groaned.
Hashem saw their tears and listened to their plea,
"I will send Moshe Rabbeinu to set My people free!"

Moshe said to Pharaoh, "Let my people go!"
But Pharaoh would not listen. He kept saying, "No! no!"
Hashem sent ten makkos — Pharaoh had no choice,
The Jews were let free, that's why we rejoice!

"We'll hear more of the story when we're at the Seder.
It's cleanup time now, and story time later.
Let's move the couch to clean what's behind,"
They all pushed together, and what did they find?

"No way!" Malka hollered, as she picked up a pouch,
"There's Meir's Haggadah, right behind the couch!"

Uncle Moishy smiled and then he explained,
"Here's another mitzvah that Malka just gained!
She found something that belonged to another,
And she gave it back to Meir, her brother!
Hashavas aveidah, it's important to learn it,
When you find something lost, make sure to return it!"

Uncle Moishy had left, it was bedikas chametz night,
When Abba would make sure there is no chametz in sight.
Once the twins were asleep and lovingly tucked in,
Mommy came down, now they're ready to begin.

Malka and Meir hid ten pieces of bread,
On top of the closet and under the bed.
Abba took a candle, a feather, and spoon,
And found all the chametz that would be burned soon.

The new day began as the alarm clock rang,
"It's Erev Pesach!" they jumped up and sang!
They rushed down the block to burn the chametz fast,
And saw their neighbor, Uncle Moishy, walking right past.

"Hi, children! I was on my way to you,
To finish preparing with the greatest crew!"
They were excited and let out a cheer,
As they waved to Riki without needing to stare.

25

Everyone was in a great pre-Pesach mood,
As they came home and smelled the yummy food.
Meir was excited to do his part,
Grating the marror is where he would start.

"Meir," said Uncle Moishy, "you're a great helper, I see,
But that's a job that's best left for me.
Because it's dangerous, it's for an adult to do,
But there are special jobs that are meant just for you!
Let's look around and see what needs to be done.
And whatever we do — we can always have fun!"

Then Meir helped Malka
at the dining room table,
Setting it nicely, as much as they were able.
They proudly put down each sparkling cup,
For the four cups of wine, they would later drink up.

Malka prepared the salt water, mixing water and salt.
She tripped and it spilled. She cried, "It's not my fault."
Uncle Moishy said, "We all make mistakes and that's okay,
Let's clean it up fast, and move on with the day."

The clock, it was ticking, time for Uncle Moishy to go.

The children would miss him — they both told him so.

"We're so glad you came. We thank you a bunch!

You saved the day and taught us so much!

You were so helpful so Mommy could rest."

They all waved goodbye, "Uncle Moishy's the best!"

The house was now ready. Time for Seder night.
Everything was clean and shining so bright.
The children ran upstairs, the hour was late,
They showered and dressed — they both looked so great!

Mommy came down, and couldn't believe her eyes.
Everything was ready, oh, what a surprise!
"What a beautiful table! So special! So grand!"
The children both kissed her. They each took a hand.

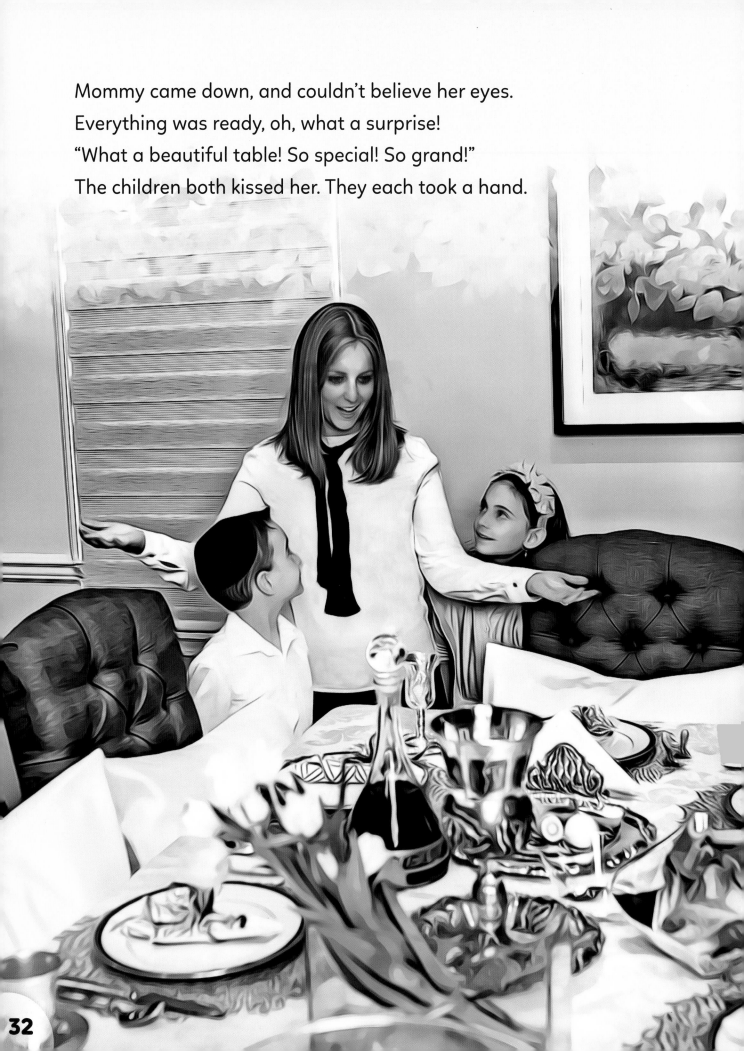

"The best surprise you made for me
Was working together so perfectly!"
Mommy lit the candles, She beamed with such pride,
Both children were smiling, standing at her side.

Malka and Meir were so pleased with each other,
They proudly smiled at their father and mother.
Now that Seder night was finally here,
They were ready to enjoy this special time of year.